# The Thief
## and other stories

**By Michael Rectenwald**

THE THIEF AND OTHER STORIES. Copyright © 2013 by Michael Rectenwald. All rights reserved. With the exception of brief quotations or passages in reviews, essays, interviews, or on radio, television, or the Internet, no part of this book may be reproduced in any form or by any means without permission from the Publisher.

ISBN-13: 978-1481181310
ISBN-10: 1481181319

APOGEE BOOKS
726 Broadway
Room 634
New York, NY 10003

# Contents

The Thief..................................................................1

Police State............................................................22

Launching Pad.......................................................29

Misery Loves Company That Hates Itself.....................37

The Moon Setting In The Dawn Of The 21st
    Century............................................................43

The D......................................................................46

The Monk................................................................50

The Storm...............................................................56

About the Author.....................................................58

He had begun to consider a method of escape from these difficulties, although they weren't really difficulties as such. They were more like a tincturing of his mind. Seemingly ineradicable, yes, but intangible, like intellectual property. He did have obligations, a wife and three kids, but these weren't the problem exactly — although otherwise he could have just walked away and become just another babbling lunatic mendicant. As a bum the inapt phrases wouldn't be out of place. For him they were an occupational hazard. But he couldn't be a bum just yet. He had things to work out first.

Arlene finally showed. The host led them to a table. Arlene was loaded with the accouterments of business. She put things down without much thought — keys, cell phone, pen and tablet — throwing them on the table. He felt sad for the things, the way she treated them. She spoke all the while. The words were apparently meant to deflect attention from her obvious vulgarity. But words made her more vulgar, he thought. She had no respect for words, treating them like commonplace verbal rubbish. She masticated while speaking, with saliva and relish. He was disgusted.

"I need something crazy," Arlene said. He thought she was talking about him. She said she needed an act, a comedian for some show.

He knew many, but he couldn't think about it now.

"No."

"Like a Jerry Boswell with a Tom Fink twist. What do you mean 'No?' But not quite, I can't put my finger on it. Something new, different. Not just the same old stuff. Know what I mean, not like just crazy antics but maybe some message in the humor. If he's not out there we'll create him. I just can't put my finger on it. I hate that. I know what I mean. I know what I'm looking for. I'd know it if I saw it."

"Yes."

"I knew you'd know what I mean. If anybody'd know

I knew you would."

"No."

This was the way he'd been conducting business for weeks now. He wasn't listening at all and had no intentions of taking any action on any answers. He was just trying to get through each conversation, as if only getting through the conversations was an accomplishment. He simply said "yes" or "no" arbitrarily.

"Of course not," she said.

"No."

"Definitely not," she confirmed.

The ice clinking in the water glasses, the sound of forks and knives on porcelain, the excessive ministrations of the waiter, the useless exchange of words — all these were excruciatingly painful to him.

"You're driving a hard bargain these days. How is your family?"

"Yes."

"What have you been doing with yourself?"

"Yes."

"Have any vacations planned?"

"Yes."

"We're going to Spain. Have you ever been? I've heard it's gorgeous."

"No."

"Maybe France? Paris?"

"No."

Arlene cross-referenced everything, looking for a hook on him.

"You get the gist of what I'm saying, it's kind of like this 'Yes-No' thing of yours, like 'No' to everything. Like 'No' to oil spills. Like 'No' to the ozone layer. That's what I'm looking for here," Arlene went back to business. "Like the 'No' comedian. The guy with the 'No' attitude, but the 'No' is kinda like … in a 'Yes' framework. Like he's really a 'Yes' man. But really what it comes down to is somebody getting up there and slamming everything, gently … and like he's unconventional but with a license to be unconventional. You know. If anyone in this business knows, you do."

He'd heard nothing but a droning sound. Arlene might as well have been an insect. Her prolixity was like a cricket tweaking. What was her being for? he thought, distractedly.

"Arlene, this is all so embarrassing to me. Please, please, spare me this *ignominy*," he said, underlining that word to hopefully extricate himself from the air filthy with catch phrases. "You make me sick." He said this more imploringly than harshly. Then he returned his face to its previous expression, hardly realizing that he'd spoken. It was as if an outside force had spoken through him, because he had no recollection of speaking the words. They were supplied.

Arlene's face contorted in obvious pain. But it wasn't so much the pain of insult as of being struck by some alien thing on the side of her head. It was a hint of a strange and negative universe, crawling with perverse, chaotic monsters, opening its jowls before her mind's eye.

"Arlene," he heard the voice saying then, "do you know where I might get hold of a large sum of money, quickly? … There's a mind that's working, but it has no interest in this empirical realm, which is regarded as inviolate. It has no interest in body language, in the feeding-and-being-fed mind. The eater. The waiter. The candle-stick-maker."

He became aware of a strange odor emanating from his body. It was the same smell that comes from bums. But it wasn't the small of garbage cans. It was the smell of his unconscious. It leaked the acrid air of barnyards, alleys, junkyards, fens, and the musty attics of his childhood, making their way into the thin afternoon light.

"You're on a another planet. You're fucking insane. But that doesn't give you the right to *insult* me? Who do you think you are?"

Arlene got up and left the table. She had looked and spoken very painfully, but he didn't recognize her any longer. She seemed to be some animated machinery with words coming out of it. What ridiculous microchip soul propelled her, and why?

He went back to his office. He played with some pencils. He was dazed, but not by Arlene. He fell asleep at his desk and dreamt about being aboard a big cruise ship flying through the sky. All the Power People were there, and everything implied that he shouldn't be, that he didn't belong, because he hadn't taken the Power seriously enough, as if it weren't real. But if it was real, the dream was to prove it, not by words, but by an ethereal force of the magnitude and consequence of the Almighty. The dream had already convicted him of the crime he was about to commit against the Power. Arlene and the other angels who were in the good favor of the Power kept admonishing him: He was a terrible wrongdoer. That was the tone.

The next few days he began thinking of ways to get the money. He looked through his bank statements to see how he'd received large sums. As an agent, money was often transferred to his account in down payments for talent performances. Part was his commission, ten to fifteen percent. When the money was in his account, he thought, all he would have to do was withdraw it, all of it, and leave. And what would he do when the client asked for the money? He'd tell them he hadn't gotten it yet. What was $50,000 compared to the national debt? Compared to what these asses make in a year? He had to keep in mind that this was just a restaurant tip and no one would miss it, or care. It was some peoples' weekend expense money. The local Boy Scout troop had a larger annual budget. And so on.

A few days later he telephoned Arlene. "Yes, I think I have that act you're looking for … the comedian. Yeah, well, I've been thinking, there's a guy doing the local club scene; I think he's perfect for what you want." Somehow he had mustered some cogency.

"Well I'm glad you've decided to play ball, Richard. Really it's about time. Don't think we all haven't noticed how crazy you've been acting. But it's all right. I'm glad you're back. Let's get this thing together." He thought he heard some trace of pity in her voice, which made him furious.

"But I need a bigger commitment, Arlene," he went on. "I need an advance on several acts. Promise me that you'll continue to work with me. I don't have an ulterior motive. I wouldn't rob you. I just need insurance. I need a *conviction*. Please work with me here. I need help." He pled and the pleas were pathetically incongruous and undermining of his argument. He continued, involuntarily multiplying misstatements, but he couldn't help it.

However, he sensed something. Paradoxically, the compilation of negatives was working in his favor, just as too many positives sometimes worked the other way.

"Of course, I know this is not *protocol*." He said this as a way to move toward closing the deal. But that word was never used in Los Angeles.

"How many acts are you talking about, exactly?"

"Ten."

Ten acts at an advance of $5,000 each meant $50,000.

"I can't believe I'm considering this. Not two days ago you basically called me an idiot. No one needs a talent agent that much. You're completely out of bounds. It's *unheard-of*. But I know you have issues. I'm trying to help."

So you see there's no wonder why he did it. Arlene was confirming it. He thought she was confirming his real, unspoken intention. Maybe it was "for all intents and purposes" the same as the spoken one. As usual, he employed his own interpretive method. No one could possibly know the meanings that he took from one's speech. He asked one question and meant another. Then he listened to the answer to check whether or not it represented an affirmation of

6

the corresponding, unspoken question. He'd established the two as equivalent. When Arlene responded affirmatively to his actual question, she answered the silent and parallel one as well.

He hated Arlene more than ever now. She actually believed that he regarded the business with the same reverence that she did. She didn't give him credit for any ambiguity. Until now, he had some minor hesitations of conscience. But no more.

He did it. After securing the deposit from Arlene, he went into the bank. Her company, the talent, the major networks, none of this crossed his mind as he entered the bank … just the teller who was extremely good- and honest-looking.

She gave him a chance to reconsider.

"Are you sure?" she asked him after he slid the withdrawal slip to her, his hand extending beneath the bars. She hesitated. He affected an air of indignation. She then counted out the bills deliberately, each bill representing another chance to change his mind. But there's no difference between one of them and all of them, he thought, as the bills became more.

There was another delay. The teller had pressed a button. She summoned a guard. The teller found no immediate reason to explain the delay, if only because by his actions he must have forfeited certain benefits. Which ones were they? he wondered. The counting had been in graduated denominations and so the sentence would be.

Finally, "Mr. Heywood," the teller spoke, "with sums of the size, of which you have just withdrawn, it is our procedure," she continued, looking up behind him, at the approaching guard, "to have you escorted from the bank … by one of our security personnel."

The explanation was rational. But he feared he might be arrested right then and there.

"But I still haven't done anything illegal," he thought, relieved as he walked freely through the lot to the car. The abiding possibility of reverting to

7

"procedure" without serious consequences allowed him to keep from reverting. When, exactly, if ever, would the line be crossed, with no turning back? It was as if the thought exonerated him. He was also exonerated by words such as "procedure" and "installments." The words made him a decent citizen and communicated the same to a quelled and believing community. They suppressed his paranoia, which would otherwise radiate and congeal as suspicion.

There was no point at which his actions could be judged and at which he could be convicted, erase the thought, no, even accused, of anything. How could any fraud be assigned? He judged these words, held them up, assigned them values: convicted equals zero, fraud equals minus one and accused equals minus two. He considered the full force of these assignments, and, as if by his own affixing, determined their weight upon him. Once handled as concepts, they would be defeated as realities. In other words, all the control resided in his head.

When he got back to the office, a message was waiting from Arlene. He poured some coffee, then dialed her. He felt indignant and thought that Arlene should be grateful that he hadn't stolen any money from her.

"I need an agreement from you that you'll use those sums for the intents and purposes for which they were deemed."

What was that? How did that phraseology get communicated to her? He didn't like the sound of it. It had to have been carried through the air like pollen. Arlene, allergic to something, felt her nose itch.

He felt badgered.

"Listen, Arlene, just because you handed me a little pile of cash doesn't mean you own me. How dare you call here harassing me? This is no big deal. This is simply an arrangement, do you understand? Things have merely been moved around in space. Things have been transferred. There's been no earth-shaking event here. What's this doggerel you're talking here?"

Arlene was momentarily silenced.

"No big deal?"

That covered only part of what outraged her. The shocking attitude he had adopted, that he insulted her again, but mostly, that there was no value anywhere. How could anyone conduct business with a whacko who valued nothing?

"Send me over paperwork to cover this," she demanded, as if her words would execute the deed.

That night he went to face the children. Maggie, his daughter, greeted him at the door, jumping up and down, sliding along his lap. She was three. Each tenderness was a pain, seeing her innocence and trust, and knowing that he, her Daddy, was now a crook, a dark character. He slinked around the house, shadowy and stealthy. He imagined that his skin complexion was somehow darker. Maybe his own prejudice about criminals was leaking into his self-image. But what if it isn't prejudice at all, but something universal, an image of the offender relegated to the shadows in the villages of our distant past, and buried deep within the collective unconscious? And now I've had tapped it! Everything up to this point had suggested itself as completely arbitrary. But here was something that presented itself as fundamental and universal.

His wife Carol stomped around the house in a desperate rage. Toys were scattered everywhere. The scent of Chinese vegetables mingled and hung in the air. Everything seemed in its place, as incongruous as it was to him. Marriage and children had generally masked his illness. But when obligations weren't stacked up to define him, his discomfiture would sometimes disclose itself before his wife's and even his oldest son's, Jaime's, eyes. These moments only seemed to augment Jaime's feelings for his father. Richard believed that Jaime's compassion was unlimited. But he knew that Carol didn't have such sympathy.

During dinner, he wanted to say something about the

crime he'd committed, but he couldn't. Sensing that words were inadequate to his torment, he started moaning. The children looked at him, amazed. After hesitating, Maggie smiled. Jaime snorted and spewed milk through his nose. The baby, Daniel, imitated the grunts to the delight of the other two. Finally all three groaned and laughed. Then Richard started laughing uncontrollably. He thought then that maybe he was normal in the biological sense, because the overall accord between him and the kids was perfect. All of our tissue and its spiritual emanation are in complete accord, he thought. Everyone is a piece of biological fate unfolding. No wonder Carol doesn't get it and the kids do.

In fact, Carol was terrified.

He wanted to watch television to escape. But he made the mistake of turning on the local news. The first story was a man being escorted to jail, hands cuffed behind, trying to head-butt the camera. The fear went through Richard's body. Back to the anchor, another crime, and a government official indicted on thirteen charges of embezzlement, fraud, extortion and conspiracy.

So, during the day, the rules of order are established and monitored, Richard thought. At night, the focus turns to those who deviate. He felt hounded already, and yelled out to Carol who was still in the kitchen.

"The entire news is about hunting criminals!"

"You've just noticed?" she answered, exasperated. And why hadn't he noticed before? he wondered.

The pretty anchor lady hated criminals, her facial expressions and intonation showed that. He looked at Maggie crouching over her plastic kitchenware and talking to her baby doll. She stroked the baby's hair and comforted her, while the prosecution vindicated itself against the reprobate. An airplane soared over the house and the sound indicted him. He now felt that the power resided with that big ugly whole — the airplanes, machine guns, tanks, prisons, police radios, televisions, cell phones, modems, and servers: everything was communicating instantly and circumspectfully, covering everything — human society reaching so far that he couldn't imagine going out to the farthest reaches and looking at the wildest, rarest flower in peace. If a policeman were to stop him in the wilderness and ask him his name, he would tell the cop that he's as anonymous as any blade of grass and the cop would scowl and search him, suspicious from the first, because all humans are guilty. Dostoevsky said that man was the "ungrateful biped" and that his ungratefulness differentiated him from all other creatures. But it's his guilt, Richard thought. Guilt covers a multitude of sins, and guilt precedes the sin, as it did in his case, because the guilt he felt at being at odds with the environment, actually feeling guilty for finding it ludicrous, made his crime possible. He'd already believed he was in the wrong and he simply had to validate it. He was the bastard and no one should need to answer to him. Who was he to so insist that anyone live up to his so-called higher expectations? He was the anomaly and anything foreign to the system was, in biology, the sickness. And so he'd felt guilty. He felt guilty for having imaginarily crushed people mentally, denigrating them, bringing them to their proverbial knees, and, because he was a beneficent god, pulling them back up to their feet, dusting them off, and returning them, in all his mercy, their dignity as human beings — but not before they had acknowledged their inferiority and stupidity and short-comings, knowing that their minds revolved in such short range, knowing full well their planetary insignificance and the blight that they had done to him on account of their ignorance. It was this guilt that now allowed him to so easily adapt to being the criminal. These thoughts flowed freely out of him, as if having been there all the while, as if he had been expected by them, as if this moment were always waiting.

For some hours, he sat on the easy chair gazing absently at the television. The floodgates opened and everything rushed in. He was at the full disposal of the environment. He slept like that, his mind an open wound through which anything and almost everything might flow. His body was feverish the whole time while the monsters had their way with the vesicle. There were no dreams to report, there was no organizing element, simply a flourishing of chaos and the outer space having its way in an otherwise selective inner space. A deafening silence had a definite pitch, and characterless being had a definite character. Simply put, the universe revealed an intentionality, an ethereal force which communicated, not through words, but more intimately, as if from within the essence to which it wished to communicate.

    He woke the next morning in a very mechanical state of mind. Everything was boiled away except for facts, which had to be dealt with. What was he going to do? The thought of killing Arlene crossed his mind, and now he knew how people got to the point of murder. He thought of just brushing her away like a gnat. Having faced the absolute, with its absolute intention, everything else seemed rather mechanical, relative, insubstantial, papier-mâché, and absorbed back into the ultimate in quick and easy order. But he knew not everyone would see it that way. His act would appear as an absolute offense to the absolute. A big deal.

    Then he thought of doing nothing but allowing time to pass, letting the thing "cool off" as he eventually put it to Carol. He did let days pass. Weeks. He didn't dare do any work. He went into his office and just touched things, afraid of the defiled papers, shuffling stacks, then left. Everything was spoiled. Only now when he'd ruined everything did he recognize any inherent value in anything. He looked at old contracts — the "talent" that he'd despised now didn't seem so stupid. It now superseded its mere timeliness. The names looked at him as if they were immortal classics, the vengeance of the immediate against his over-blown sense of history, which had always been a defense against annihilation. The more he had resented kowtowing to the stars, the more he plunged into "great art and literature," neglecting everything else. But it had never really worked. I never really could exist in the world, he thought, as if he'd somehow left it, as if he'd gotten his wish to be removed.

Carol's mother, Bridget, came in from the east coast. She was a woman of very modest, yet independent means, who never really had to work a day in her life. She had arrived in the midst of all this, expecting a site-seeing vacation on the Hollywood lots. Her timing was always pitiful. But her problem wasn't solely a matter of timing. She always expected to be the center of attention. Likewise, her presence was inevitably regarded as importunity. He couldn't bring himself to acknowledge her. He moved around her in the house, his eyes focused on nothing, glazed over. After a few days, she said that she just couldn't stand the tension. He had no idea what she was talking about.

Carol had been desperate about his condition. The lack of sense was exhausting and demoralizing. Although things were growing clearer for him, he couldn't tell her about that. She thus saw no difference between his current and previous state.

Bridget began sulking, and eventually would have no more of it. "I'll just leave!" she announced. He was hit with a sidelong sadness and pity. There's no world for her either, he thought, nor Carol, nor the kids. Our little grouping of pathetic creatures, the children wonderful and vibrant yet prohibited from life somehow, by me, by the world. John, Carol's father, a drunkard; I am an alien; Bridget, shattered by divorce; and Carol, lost in the middle of it all.

Bridget dropped a hint about taking a trip to San Francisco and Carol joined in. They would all go but him. He was relieved.

Arlene hadn't called him for two and a half months. He was almost convinced that this meant she knew what he'd done and somehow approved of it, was looking the other way, understood his mental condition, and that, in effect, she was suggesting that he should have taken the money. He even went so far as to imagine that Arlene had designed the whole caper. Anything rather than bear the idea that Arlene was like a plotting little rat in her corner, conspiring with lawyers, a materialistic grubber, concocting the worst of calumnies and vengeance against him. Hadn't she imagined how he was with his daughter, a distillation of the most rarefied air of beauty, or was she, like a collection agent, appraising him in terms of his debt alone, casting him in the basest form possible, extracting only one point of reference from the whole of his existence?

At that point some kind of writ must have been drawn up, containing something he'd thought it almost impossible to contain, taken as he was by the idea that he had inviolate rights of some sort, even though he was a criminal. But when necessary, he realized, the forces could draw up anything that suited them, devising laws as they went along, making statements and getting orders to say what they wanted. There is no doubt that in an effort to gain, save or recapture some money that a conspiracy of actors will take shape and develop around a locus of justification, endowing that justification with the fullest extent of force available; will see to it life is never given value above property.

"Your house has been repossessed." He was minutes away from home on the way back from the office. The words were audible in his head. He drove on, relieved for some reason, singing along with the song on the radio, "These Are The Good Old Days." He noticed several bums lining the sidewalks.

Once on his street he saw from the car items that somehow looked familiar, like things closely associated with his life, on the lawn. Oh, it's our furniture and stuff, he thought, casually at first. Then he imagined that Carol was following through on one of her threats.

Approaching the door with an aim to cop a desperate plea with her, he found a lock box on the door handle. The house was empty. The windows were naked. The hardwood floors looked at him, disclaiming, even scorning him. The children's toys had been carelessly thrown on the porch.

"Arrest me but leave my children alone!" he screamed inside.

The living room where he'd wrestled with Jamie, hugged and kissed him and his sister, and Daniel, fought with yet loved his wife, was now abruptly vacated, violated and simply ransacked. A church came to his mind, the sacrilege done to statues, and the general opprobrium with which such acts are regarded. Yet here was one of the only remaining sanctuaries on earth, where he'd known the holiest of moments, if anything could be called holy, and all force was not only accepted but morally sanctioned in its desecration, granted that someone's money, money backed by a serious institution, was at stake. At the same time knew he was being sentimental, and laughed at himself, at that bit of sermonizing, how quickly he too could adopt the moral hypocrisy.

The house had been seized by court order. Carol and the children were due back tomorrow. She'd been gone now for months.

He went immediately to his office for the money. There was $47,000 left in the safe. He'd spent $3,000 in the course of paying some office bills. He took the money and drove to the nearest police station. He had to drive around in many circles to find it ... and to the first policeman behind the glass, he confessed, pushing the money toward the cop. He continued by telling him how he had been distressed to the point of insanity, but that he should not be let off, just let his wife and kids have the house back, that he should not like to plead insanity, but just take the sentence "straight up." That's the phrase he used, "straight up," as if the

15

cop were a bartender. The bartender image entered his mind, and he thought, he'll serve you all right.

A rush of panic came over him as he realized that he'd spoken as if he could actually order whatever justice he wanted. What a mistaken idea. What if I've confessed under this false assumption? he thought. The panic swelled. The whole scene felt scripted, like lines that had been rehearsed by the unconscious. He felt like "the universal criminal." This was the archetypal confession scene. But it also felt like "the universal confusion of the cop with the bartender scene."

The cop looked at him in astonishment, told him to wait, went back into the offices, and left him standing there. He couldn't believe that he was left alone with no guards. What if he should run, or worse, injure, or kill someone? He'd always had thoughts like that. Walking into a lobby of a hotel or office building, he would think, why are they letting me walk through here of my own accord — what if I had a gun?

Richard heard the cop laughing along with another officer behind the half-open door. He heard fragments like, "well what'll I do with 'em," and "a real crack pot." There was a long delay. He imagined that he should feel insulted at being made to wait.

It was dreadfully quiet.

He waited over an hour. Meanwhile other offenders were brought in and hurried along to the side hallways. Decent people on the other side of the law came in and filed complaints and pressed charges. One lady smiled at him as she waited after filing a complaint. No one took him to be a criminal, which made him feel worse. What if I was actually a decent, basically good person who mistook himself for the other kind and balefully committed himself to that? he thought …

"God, what an awful lot," he whispered, thinking of himself, while at the same time a very disturbed, frothing man in torn clothes with a bleeding nose was pushed through the lobby with hands cuffed behind his back. This man's crime was having thrashed out for being cast in such a figure — impecunious and with such an ugly face, scarred and pockmarked and disfigured. And now he was being doubly punished. Life with its one-two punches, Richard thought, and noticed the lady smiling at him again.

He had an awful insight then into his error that came by way of that thought, life with its one-two punches. The thing is to turn the other cheek, he thought, whatever the pain. This is how to escape fate's double bind, to escape the eternal return of circumstance … But that's not true, he countered: the finite will keep repeating itself simply because it's finite. What else can happen? He thought about scenes that kept recurring, with slightly different layers, but through these layers one could find the same elements as in other scenes. He would suddenly notice the landscaping around a house, for example, and swear that he'd seen it before, in similar circumstances, yet something was different. He was older, and life was more complicated. Then he would yearn for simpler times, wistfully trying to grasp back through the additional layers, only to become exasperated. The new, amending and immediate circumstances were inexorable. This made it harder and harder to move freely, to act deliberately. Perhaps this inertia caused him eventually to effect more drastic ends. He had acted as if the end of this desperate act was not foreseeable — blindly, as if some mysterious objective could be achieved, throwing fate to the wind. But the return was there, somehow to his surprise.

The first policeman never came back. Another one came out. He figured this one must have been a specialist in his kind of crime. He wore plain clothes and was holding a computer print out. He kept looking down at the sheet, somewhat dolefully. The sheet had very little printing on it, a fact that upset Richard even further. Look how clean your record was, he thought. What a shame you've ruined it.

The detective introduced himself as "Sergeant Yoke." Averting his eyes, he asked Richard to follow him into "the examining room." The words "examining room" had somewhat of a soothing effect, as if his were a medical or psychological, rather than criminal case, as if the prospect of being diagnosed and treated was worth all the trouble he'd gotten himself into. Then the image of the doctor increased his panic. Don't tell me I did all this just to get professional attention, he thought.

"Sir," Sergeant Yoke started, coming out of his shell. "If you came here to confess a crime, you'll have to restate your confession now, but I've got to tell you that I'll have to tape record it. The problem, though, he continued, now somewhat amusedly, is a kind of technicality..."

The detective stopped short, apparently thinking through the problem of this technicality. The technicality included his little speech as well. The detective gestured like an affected professor meeting with a student, carefully considering all of the subtleties of the subject, and overly enjoying the machinations of his mind. He was also asking the student's indulgence for the considerations at hand, and asking him to join him in the enjoyment of nuances. The student felt tempted to entertain himself with the professor, when he remembered his reading. But he recalled that the detective wasn't trying to gain his confidence in order to trick out a confession. He'd come to confess in the first place. The detective was frankly asking his indulgence and admitting to a problem in the law. He wanted Richard's sympathy.

"The thing is," he resumed, "is that I can't arrest you without a confession, and yet I can't read you your Miranda rights until I'm about to arrest you. But I can't let you confess without first offering you the benefit of having a lawyer, which is really a part of the Miranda. So really I should arrest you first, if for nothing else than reading you the Miranda. Then again you really haven't legally confessed yet, so why should I arrest you? So you really have a choice here. You could leave here right now. Of course we wouldn't leave it at that. We'd send over an investigator to see if there are any grounds for an arrest, and if there were, we'd arrest you at that point. Then you could fulfill this confession need, and the case against you would be more substantial. The other choice…"

If Sergeant Yoke had at first tried to prune his speech, he finally gave up and simply spat it out whole. He'd spoken as if Richard simply shared with him an interest in an impartial execution of the law. The phrase "this confession need" modified that a bit. But the fact that Richard would be the object of that impartial execution seemed barely to have crossed the detective's mind.

"Well, there really is no other choice," he concluded. Richard wasn't satisfied. He wanted to know what was going on.

"And what about my house?" he demanded, "How could they have just seized my house like this? Is this the civil side of the same thing, or did you people do this?"

"I don't know what you're talking about," the sergeant said, growing annoyed.

"I mean, is that legal, just taking my house like that?"

"That depends on why it is being taken."

"What do you mean, you don't *know* why?" Richard asked, growing even more alarmed.

"You're saying that your house was taken and in connection with this?" the sergeant asked, definitely irritated. His life had just been complicated further. Richard could see him thinking about how convoluted it would be to track all of this.

"It sounds like you need a lawyer," the sergeant broke, relieved by his sudden recognition and cracking a smile, which wasn't really malicious.

That does me no good, Richard thought.

"That doesn't help me," he snapped, as if the sergeant were there to ease his mind, to help him. The detective actually assumed this role for a few minutes, telling him to ask someone he trusted to help him find a lawyer, that he should tell the lawyer everything, without exception, and so on. Richard thought then that the detective and this proposed legal advocate were in cahoots, the whole legal system was one big conspiracy, the defense and the prosecution just feeding each other business.

"Well, I guess that's all then," Richard said, standing up to go, the situation taking on aspects unlike itself, as if he'd been with a psychologist, or a car salesman, or a priest. The ball of authority was unraveling in his mind, and he was letting it unravel before them all. It was as if the guilt had been magnetized long ago and now sought its polarity. Bad thoughts, bad conscience, bad credit, all seeking to be reproached by their origins.

He walked out of the station. It was a beautiful evening, a billowing sky painting of huge bluffs. Beauty was so vivid in times of crisis. Nature mocked his distress.

Thank God for hotels, he thought. He booked a room in the Ramada in the little town center. Whether or not his bank account was frozen, the Visa was still good. The girl slid it through the magnetic slit perfunctorily and he slipped through a crack in the computer network. A hotel forgives; hotels forgive anyone, at least for a night. He was happy about staying in one. Such were the tricks played by the residual memory banks shooting little associative doses of pleasure at him, inappropriately.

He had almost forgotten the events of the day in the common whirlpool. He was suddenly thrust into the immediate present and no future existed. Tonight he had a hotel room, which was as far as it went. But the rising heat of the whirlpool flushed blood to his head and the panic swelled again. He'd given over the $47,000 to the police and it hadn't been returned. What about Carol and the kids? They had no home to come home to. Forget about me, but the kids, their toys, the furniture, everything, was all out on the street. What am I going to do about all this? And how could I have imagined that I could live for any real length of time on $50,000? I can't even live for a year on $100,000.

These thoughts did not frighten him as much as the idea that they hadn't occurred to him before. How ill forged the plan was, he thought. It was no plan at all, none that he knew of.

The next day he awoke to the thought of calling Arlene. Something was resolved during the night's sleep. He went to the office. When he arrived a message was waiting on his voice mail. Arlene's voice was quiet and kind. She had nothing to do with the seizure of the house. That was obvious. He finally realized that he'd left the mortgage unpaid for three months while Carol was away. And now he'd confessed to a crime, which hadn't officially been committed before he'd admitted to it.

All of this brought Richard to his first "status conference," after Carol and the kids had moved back to her mother's, and Richard moved into a boarding room.

Why did he destroy his life? He sometimes reasoned that his floating guilt needed a home, a meaningful and fitting anchor for its existence. You may not believe it, and rightfully so, he thought, imagining an audience of cynics. You may deny that any feelings need justification, convinced that no fantasies deserve action. In that case, you can walk around the way you are and keep denying them. But as for me, I've acted and forged a destiny. I've met with my fate and committed an act connected to my imaginings.

# Police State

I woke up, unusually hung-over. I gathered my clothes from the floor beside the bed, dressed, found the bathroom, and looked in the mirror. My eyes were an unbroken red. My face was pallid and green. My hair stood on end. I'm too old for this shit, I thought. I reached for a brush, wet it under the faucet, and tried to pat it down. It wouldn't lie. Forget it. I went to the kitchen and found my overcoat on the back of a chair. I slipped it on, checked for the keys and wallet, and put up the collar because it had been cold. I looked around the apartment, and seeing it empty, said goodbye forever. But then I went back through the unlocked apartment door, back into bathroom, to the medicine cabinet. For some reason, in an apartment of all women, or so I thought I'd heard, there was nothing but Viagra. I don't need that, I thought. Not that I had performed well the night before. I hadn't. I was far too drunk. But I wanted something for the morning. The only thing on offer would be coffee, I realized, and immediately thought of the coffee-shop-bookstore in Dupont Circle.

I hadn't been walking for more than five minutes before I saw several police cars. Naturally, I feared they were all looking for me. I forged through the cold thin air, trying to quell my fear with the thought that I was really just a decent person walking to a coffee-shop-bookstore, a good neighborhood establishment, despite a few radical books. After getting lost in every possible direction, I finally found it. As I reached for the door, a police car came to a stop beside me and the cop turned and looked right at me.

I suddenly felt nauseous. A metallic taste flooded my mouth. Time and space were reduced to a pinpoint, history disappeared, and I existed only as a bodily moment in fixed relation to an absolute concrete particular, namely in this case, as in others, a cop. I retched violently, several times. Puke splattered on the sidewalk and splashed onto the glass front of the coffee-shop-bookstore.

The cop presently parked the car and got out to investigate. With the usual huge range of exaggerated motion, he pulled his body out of the car in a wide arc. This was great. Right in front of the mind refinery, my mouth ajar and dripping puke, I was to face the Neanderthal, monolithic prehistory of man, the protector of idiot regimes. Just then the fancy notion I'd had of milling about in the hip bookstore seemed a foolish, trivial and banned frivolity.

My fear was not simple. I'd been so drunk the night before, I was sure I was still legally drunk now. Also I'd *said* certain things, which compounded my paranoia. I now had no clear idea of what I'd been saying, but my statements might have been construed as terroristic threats. Who knows? Of course it was all meaningless drunken banter.

But the problem was more material than that. I was on probation and any subsequent arrest would reactivate the original felony conviction and sentence. I really thought I had to have a new driver's license and was arrested in Florida for giving false testimony trying to get one. My crime was making false tongue movements. I had not yet been convicted of a felony. I'd plea-bargained for a misdemeanor, pled guilty to take the lesser charge and sentence. At the time, I'd made my living as an advertising salesman. My original crime was speeding: 30 miles per hour in a 25 mile-an-hour zone. Ninety bucks. I didn't pay. They suspended me — an abstract hanging. Then I got stopped again, this time ticketed for speeding *and* driving without a license. Luckily, they didn't notice or care that I was high on cocaine. But driving on a suspended license alone added another year to the suspension and compounded the fines. Two years later, having a suspended license and about to lose my job, I drove to Florida to apply for a new license. An ad agency friend of mine had told me that Florida was the ticket.

I told the officers at the Florida DMV that I had lived in New York City my entire adult life and had never needed to drive.

For the past eighteen years? (I was now 34).

Yes.

They asked me over and over, incredulously, at every checkpoint: Have you ever had a license?

Never.

Nice job on the written part, she said. Now for the operation of the motor vehicle. I drove around the course like an innocent 16-year-old boy. I passed everything.

Seated in front of the camera, I smiled as directed. The photographer smiled back — especially after the cop popped up from behind the curtain and cuffed me, dumping my effects into a brown paper bag. Later, I stood before a different camera for another photo I.D. This one would gain me notoriety.

The cop held all my personal possessions, listed everything on a sheet, called my attention to one at a time, as I sat in the back of the car with my hands cuffed behind my back. He was friendly. He said he'd cut me a break. Instead of taking me into the jailhouse to itemize my immediate belongings, he'd let me stay here in the car, sitting on my wrists, while the metal dug in. He commiserated with me, telling me how this was such a bitch of a way to go, just to get a damn license, pointing to the otherness of Law over which no one had any control. Even he, the cop, had no control.

Under arrest, in the pinpoint of the here-and-now, where all history ceases to be, I was outside myself, sensing this person who was in captivity and under a threat of some kind. I was removed from this flesh creature, which sweated and twisted his wrists. The static of the two-way radio went on and off, on and off.

The kinetic network of information and judgment, it occurred to me just then, the Law, descended from the apes and theology of the Bible, this Being, this Otherness, wholly created by humans in their sleep, was their God. An image had been buried in my mind's deepest recesses, a something somehow feared ultimately; I now had discovered it in the reality of the Law, which matched it. I was driven from jail to jail, riding in the wagon cage, as the paddy wagon dropped off other prisoners. I recalled having seen the paddy wagons when I'd driven behind them. They'd never appear the same to me again.

I didn't know it at the time, but Florida was one of few states in the country where making false statements to obtain a driver's license was regarded as a felony.

Now standing over a puddle of my own puke, the puke having emanated from my body, I being the perpetrator of said puke, the cop arrived on the scene to investigate. The memory of my previous arrest didn't so much as flash in my mind as seize it, as if a huge metal truck overcame my senses, injecting the metallic taste into my mouth and fluid metal into my veins. Wait, all I did was throw up. No, no, I was more than a puker.

As the cop approached me, a clerk from the bookstore came out, disgusted. This was going to cost them customers, the clerk said. I am now a crook of culture, I thought. You fucking poser, I said under my breath. I had always hated bookstore clerks. I thought that they were the same as the clerks at Bloomingdale's — pretentious little snobs who need their faces rubbed in shit.

The cop didn't care to gander at what had been the contents of my stomach. Rather, he looked *me* over. I stood there, the suspect, this weightless body in an overcoat, like a test-tube that this cop-scientist held and tilted around for his bemusement. I heard the two-way radio going off and on and off and on — the static of hell. The cop asked for some I.D.

Well. Well. See, I don't have a license, see, officer, sir, officer, sir.

The only thing I had was an invalid, ten-year-old college I.D. I pulled it out from my wallet and handed it to him. He looked at it, at me, and then smirked, as if sizing up my life as a pathetic waste. Then he stepped away with what felt like the last remains of my youth, guarding the card as if to prevent me from my reasserting my own identity. He pulled out his pocket radio and started making noises into it. People who had intended to enter the bookstore slowed down then kept walking, while the clerk stood there silently hoping for an arrest. Presently, somebody came out from the store with a mop and bucket to clean me off the street.

After a few minutes, the cop stepped toward me again. Just as he did, I noticed for the first time a long, ugly, singular hair growing out of a wart on his chin. I quickly tried to rub this particularly repulsive indication of animal transience out of my mind, knowing he had the power of God. He reached inside his jacket. I had a sudden fear that he was going to pull a gun and shoot me right there. But it was this little tube with a rubber end, a peculiar device for a man in his position to be carrying, I thought. It seemed more like a feminine device.

This is a Breathalyzer test, he announced, as if referring to my entire life as such. A Breathalyzer test. That's all it amounted to. Things that otherwise had been indefinite and nebulous now had such concrete finality. The policeman and his tube. Outside the bookstore, the cop answered whatever questions might be extant about the nature of this particular reality: it's a Breathalyzer test. Forget all those books inside there. This is what matters. Any questions? Good.

But first I was to do pirouettes with my eyes shut and index finger on my nose, instead of the top of my skull. I was to perform, right in front of all the trendy intellectuals, some of whom now gathered outside to watch.

But they didn't represent the cutting edge of knowledge; the cop did. The cop was it. Everybody else was just wasting their time, and his. The cop explained the procedures with eloquence and proper terminology. I had to give up completely.

I shut my eyes and went through conniptions, like a caged ape. I was just a functioning physical body. There was no person in me. I performed for the crowd and my master as he called out the instructions.

Then I blew into the tube. My mouth puckered and filled with air. I didn't give a shit. Let them have it, my breath, if they wanted it, I thought. How it mattered what I put in my own private test tube I couldn't figure, except perhaps that the tube was not my tube after all. They wanted to know just what was in my body. That's what the officer said, glancing over toward the other police cars that had now begun to arrive. I must have presented a significant threat. They had to take me to the station. I was over the legal limit in alcohol content, by a hair. I compulsively sneaked a glance at the long hair on his face just as he said that, hoping that he didn't notice.

He didn't cuff me, just pushed me into the back seat. He was talking on his radio about other matters up there. I realized I meant nothing at all to the cop, or, in the cop's estimation, to anyone else. Then it occurred to me that they were going to draw blood. I suddenly became worried about all the antihistamines I'd taken. My sinuses had been stuffed for about twenty-five years. Mass poisonings were vastly rewarded, and I was the criminal.

But at this point, I was confused. Did I mean anything, or didn't I? If I didn't matter, why did they bother? I thought it must be just a matter of scientific curiosity, like checking the temperature, or the chemical content of a river. They just wanted to know how polluted things were. The problem was, though, they might do something to *me* over what was in my body. So I heard my voice ask if he might forget this whole thing.

Couldn't we just drop it? I heard my voice saying. No sooner than they'd left my mouth, the sounds themselves meant nothing. They were just noises, nothing more.

I don't think so, buddy, he said casually.

Then I just sat quietly back there, like some little tenderized piece of meat. I was a soft little quietness compared to these people and their radio noises. I got myself back. I felt good about myself: I was good. I felt like a flower. I had nice, petal-like thoughts and velvety, silky feelings. I was a beautiful little thing. After all, I was filled with blood. And blood was goodness, I thought. Red goodness. I watched my blood fill up the tube. I felt like crying that they drew it out of me, just like that, and it was leaving me, for good. They took that part of me and ran it through tests.

Subject is waiting for the results of blood tests, my officer said through his two-way, as I sat in the station on the emergency-room-like bed with gauze taped on my arm. I accepted as fact that anything I might dream up could happen. I came clean.

# Launching Pad

I was going to pick up my second wife's stepdaughter of her third marriage. That was supposed to feel normal. That is, according to my second wife, my second ex. She didn't exactly say that it was supposed to feel normal. That was just how she sounded on the telephone. Meet her at the airport, she said. It was her habit, telling people what to do. That was the best thing about our marriage. She told me what to do. Since I didn't know what to do, somebody had to tell me. It was good that she did.

How did I get into these things? I thought, as I stood beside the bathtub, waiting for the shower to get hot. She called me, said that her stepdaughter was coming to town. She was coming to look at a school. What did that mean, "Look at a school?" I thought about that when she said it, "Look at a school." Maybe she was a demolition expert, sizing it up and figuring where to put the dynamite? Or a painter? But I knew what it meant. She was thinking of going there to college. When I hesitated, she said, well, you're not working are you? What she meant to say was that I wouldn't be too busy, would I? But she never said things that way. She had to put some spin on the ball, "You're not working are you?" She said Julie didn't know anyone else in Pittsburgh, could I meet her and let her stay at my place a couple days? She said, you know, it's Julie, Frank's youngest. Frankly, I didn't. But what did it matter? As for the working, I was, and I wasn't. But I wasn't going to try and explain that to her. She never cared to understand before.

When I said I was "going to pick her up," I meant I was going to drive to the airport to meet her. I agreed to do it. And now here I was getting ready to go. I took a shower, and got dressed. Then I decided I better clean up a bit. I emptied the ashtrays and threw out some newspapers. I gathered up my dirty clothes and put them on the floor of my closet. The place was as close as it was going to get to a college dormitory. My second ex had called on Thursday, and now it was Saturday. Short notice, I thought. What did she expect, fresh paint?

It was getting near time to go. I decided to have some coffee first, and went into the kitchenette. I took out the old grinds from the coffee maker, threw them in the trash, and put in a new filter. I loaded four scoops in. Then I stood holding the thing and looking at the fresh grinds a few seconds, almost absently. The dope. I'd forgotten to hide the dope. It was on top of the turntable, on the dresser in living room/bedroom. I went in and put it in the underwear drawer. I figured she wouldn't be looking in there. I wonder if college kids still smoke the stuff? I thought. I went back and poured water into the coffee machine. I stood there watching the coffee drip into the glass pot. Then I thought, don't just stand there; get your cup ready. I opened the cupboard where I knew the cups were, and picked up one of the bigger ones. This particular cup had writing on it. It had the word "Navy" on it, beside a figure of some kind of ram holding an anchor. I never thought about it before, but now I wondered what I was doing with this cup. I never went to Navy, nor did I know anyone who did. Oh well, I thought, it's a coffee cup just the same. I filled the cup a little over half full, and added some powdered cream. I started drinking the coffee when I realized I didn't have time to stand there drinking coffee; I had to get going.

Half way to the airport I started thinking about where I was going to park the car while I went in to the baggage claim area to meet the girl. I'll just leave it outside the door on the baggage claim level, I thought. Then I realized that I'd left the little piece of paper with the airline and flight information back at the apartment. Damn it, it's too late to go back. I know the flight arrives at 12:05, I thought, but I don't remember which airline. I'll have to drive around the baggage claim level, I thought. I'll just keep circling till I find her. When she doesn't find me inside, she'll come outside looking. She's tall and thin, with long jet-black hair. You can't miss her. That's what she said.

I got to the airport and followed the signs to the arrival area. I drove slowly around the semicircle, looking for the tall dark girl. I started worrying after five or so laps. Where the hell is she? I thought. After a couple more laps, I parked the car, and got out. I was starting to get mad. How on earth do I get into such things? Then I started worrying for the girl. She was probably upset. Well, in case she doesn't know it yet, the world's not perfect. I walked back and forth outside. I looked in each door. After about ten minutes of doing this, I went inside. I looked at my watch. It was 12:45.

I looked for a moving conveyor belt. The one on the very end was still moving. There were a couple of suitcases all by themselves going around in circles. When I got to the baggage conveyor, I looked up at the lighted sign. It read: USAIR FL 325. Then I remembered. This was the flight. I rushed around looking for the girl, not really seeing anything I was looking at. Then I noticed a pair of legs of a person whose upper body was hidden by a telephone cubicle. Even in the middle of this minor panic, I couldn't help looking at these legs. They were the legs of a woman. They were gorgeous. Moreover, they were bare — no stockings. That is something an older man likes, I thought, bare legs. What are you doing thinking about these legs right now? There's a girl missing, I reminded myself.

I walked in a wide arc around this baggage stile, trying to see 180 degrees at a time. I retraced this semicircle a couple times. Then I stopped in my tracks at the top center of the arc and just stared without looking at anything. I was on the other side of the phones. I looked at what was attached to the legs. There were some very shapely hips, and long wavy black hair that nearly reached the waistline. It was the girl. I stood there facing her back. She held the phone to her ear, waiting. She wasn't talking. She was in white denim shorts that fit tightly, wrapped with a very narrow belt around a diminishing waist. I couldn't believe it! This was little Julie who was going to be staying with me for a couple days in my no-bedroom apartment.

There was a nervous hesitation in my body as I approached to tap her on the back. My limbs sputtered. I felt like some jerk needlessly asking a strange woman for a light of his cigarette. But I put it in my head: you're the elder who's going to look after this young girl. She's relying on your kindness and experience.

She turned around, without a hint of being startled. She stood there, looking blankly at me, not thinking about what was in front of her eyes. She was thinking about what she was hearing, or not hearing, in the phone.

"Are you Julie," I asked.

After a few seconds she realized that I was he, the guy sent to pick her up.

"Oh … Michael!" she said.

"Yeah, I'm … Michael." I was thinking of saying more, that I was hers or one of her stepmother's ex-husbands. That is, of her stepmothers, I was one ex-husband of one, Glenda, in particular. Of Glenda's three ex-husbands, I was her first, to be exact. But Glenda was my second wife. I have two ex-wives, and I'm married to a third, although, of course, we're separated.

I skipped it. I was a bit surprised to hear this girl call me Michael, though. I didn't know what she'd call me. I hadn't thought about it. But now I thought she might have called me Uncle Mike. Or Mr. Becker. I liked it that she'd called me Michael. I've always thought that was the affectionate version of my name. I didn't mind her being affectionate with me. But I was nervous.

"I'm sorry I'm late," I said. "You were probably worried."

She tilted her head ever so slightly to one side, and threw her hair back behind her shoulder. She laughed and said, "I didn't *think* I'd be stood up."

"Good," I said, "Because I had the hardest time finding the right baggage area. I just couldn't find it.

"Do you have any bags?"

"Yeah, they're over there." She pointed to the baggage conveyor belt. Hers were the two bags going around by themselves. I felt worse, thinking those abandoned bags were hers.

"Well let me get them. My car's right outside. We'll try to make this a good stay for you."

"Oh, I'm sure it will be a good time," she said.

I rushed over to the conveyor belt and chased the bags and grabbed them before they had a chance to turn the corner to the other side. They felt like a hundred pounds each. I hoisted them off, and scooted over beside her. I hurried along, pointed with my head and told her my car was outside over this way; let's go out this door over here. The bags were so heavy that my arms were fully extended, and I had to hunch my shoulders. I scurried along with short, pained steps. I watched her walking beside me. She was gliding along, with just the right length of step. There was absolutely no wind resistance against her perfectly smooth, tan, supple body.

When we got through the automatic door, I said, do you mind waiting just one second? I had felt my hair sliding and was afraid my bald spaces might be showing. I sat the bags down, as if I were merely resting. I ran my hands through my hair, trying not to be noticed. I figured I might as well tuck my shirt in while I was at it. The old fitted oxford cloth was tight around my waist. I must look ridiculous, I thought. I felt awkward next to her.

I picked the bags back up. I turned my head slightly to look over at her. She smiled at me. I thought that I must have been misinterpreting things. The smile appeared seductive. She's probably just humoring you, dummy, I thought. Young girls don't mean anything with a smile like that. She doesn't know what the hell she's doing. She's trying to make you feel better.

On the way back to the apartment I felt a tense silence in the car. I didn't know what on earth to say or do. What was I supposed to do? I thought maybe I should show her around the city. But then I thought, she's not here for *you* to show her around. You're just giving her a place to stay. It's not your place to do anything more. I couldn't help sneaking looks at her legs. They were so young and fresh. They were naked. I wonder if she knows this? I thought. Could she know the madness this put in a man's mind? At such an age? Does she have to be so damn friendly? What's she doing being so friendly? I looked at her; she smiled. I looked back to the road. I looked back to her; she smiled again. It was too much. I felt myself starting to get mean. I had to be mean. It was the only way I could feel. If I felt anything else I'd have been a fool. But now I was feeling like a mean fool. How else could you act in such a situation, when a girl's too friendly and attractive for her own good?

Finally she spoke, as if to break the ice. "What do you think of Chatham College?"

I didn't think anything of Chatham College. I couldn't think of anything to say, never having had a single thought about it. I tried hard to think of something. Nothing was on the top of my mind. I grew tense trying to think. It was an all-women's school. That's good, I thought.

"It's an all-women's school," I said, "That's good." I took another look at her legs. That's good, I thought. It's an all-women's school.

I never thought of myself as a failure. But here was this beautiful girl, Frank's youngest, asking me what I thought about schools. And just now I thought that might not be such a good idea. I mean, with three wives, and ten times that many jobs behind me, and four kids living away, two in a step home, and two in a double step home ... When Glenda and I split, our two kids, Michelle and John went with her. They lived for a while with her, and eventually with her and her second husband, Tom. Then she met Frank. When she divorced Tom for Frank, the kids, Michelle and John, ended up going to Tom. That's the double step home. My first two kids, Michael and Elizabeth, live with their mother, Rita, my first wife, and her second husband, Pete.

"Well, I just thought, you know. I heard you were a professor, so I thought you knew about schools and stuff."

Julie said this as if sensing what I'd been thinking. Glenda must have told her that. That I was a professor. I was never a professor. I happened to have taught Art in a few universities. That hardly made me a professor. That was like Glenda. She enhanced the positions of people that she knew. That made some kind of difference to her.

I thought about explaining that the quality of the schools I taught at didn't matter to me, that I took teaching jobs just to earn money, and what I cared about was my work. Then I thought, don't tell her that. The kid hasn't even started college yet. I was more nervous now. This went beyond the shape of my apartment. It was about being more than a place for Julie to stay. I hoped she wasn't looking to me to show her the school. I didn't say anything for now. I didn't want to shatter any hopes. About school, or anything else.

I told her, Yeah, I'm sure Chatham's a good school.

We arrived at my apartment.

We're here, I said, and got out to get her bags out of the trunk. By the time I had the bags in hand, Julie was at the door waiting for me to let her in. I carried the bags to the door and looked at her. I sat the bags down and pulled the keys from my pants pocket. I inserted the key, and turned. I pushed the door open. Julie walked in. She seemed to be very comfortable, like she wasn't a guest, but someone who'd been in my apartment before.

"It smells like something's burning," she said. She was already in the kitchenette. "Michael, you left the coffee on!"

Julie went over to the coffee maker and pulled the plug. A black sludge sizzled on the bottom of the glass pot.

"I'm going have to clean this out," she said, holding up the pot to show me.

I hauled the bags into the living-room/bedroom. Julie took to cleaning out the pot with a scrub brush. I felt bad that she had just arrived and was already cleaning my pot.

And that my opinion about things counted to her. And that this place was perhaps the launching pad for her future.

When she was done, I apologized for the condition of the apartment. She said there was nothing to he sorry for. I told her there was only the couch bed, so I'd sleep on the floor. She said there was no reason for me to sleep on the floor. She said we could share the bed. I trust you, she said, laughing.

I wondered what the woman had in mind. Glenda, that is. Did she think she owed me something? Or, that I owed her? Was she trying to set me up? Or, was Frank looking for a good reason to kill me? Glenda had no reason to set me up. I didn't have anything. And Frank couldn't care much less if I lived or died. I think I only saw him once. No, the thing was, Julie was to look at a school. And I was supposed to be a professor.

# Misery Loves Company That Hates Itself

My wife and I had had a fight. It was nine o'clock Sunday morning. I had already taken a friend to the airport, read the newspaper, run five miles, and searched the want ads for a new job. Just back from my run in the woods, I was high. I felt like Pan, the god of nature — all legs, like a satyr.

When I returned to the house, I re-read the classified ad I'd circled. Now my wife woke and came downstairs.

"Listen to this want ad," I said. I read her the ad for a freelance writer.

"Good, go for it," she said. She yawned. She went to the kitchen to pour coffee. I followed.

"Yeah, I think I'll send them a couple short stories, maybe that one about the girl in the airport. Know which one I mean?"

"There you go again, Jack, the same damn mistake again. The job is writing television scripts, and you're gonna send them poetry."

"I didn't *say* poetry. I said I was sending short stories. That's two different things, in case you don't know."

"You know what I mean. Your fiction is just like poetry. You should send something normal, like an essay. Send something that shows you can write a goddamn sentence."

"What in the hell do you mean by *that*? My fiction tells simple stories," I pleaded.

"You're always out of touch with things. You should send an essay that shows you write a damn sentence. Trust me on this; you don't know what's going on out there. Write an essay."

She was disqualifying the hundreds of pages I'd written to this point. Of course, with her high-school education, she was entitled.

"I'll tell you something, Glenda," I said, my voice rising. When I get up to accept my Pulitzer Prize, I won't be thanking my loving wife. I'll say, 'Thanks to my wife, for fucking fucking me all the way! The fucking bitch! Impeding me …'"

I was reduced to a stammer. If you have to argue your art into acceptance, forget it, it's over. And everybody's the goddamn critic. The guy on the street, who can barely read the newspaper, suddenly becomes a literary critic when he finds out you write and he manages to worm one out of you.

She smirked. The thought didn't pose a terrible threat of lost possibility.

"Who in the hell are you to tell me what to send? Where do you get off as the expert all of the sudden?" I yelled. "Get out of here, get out of the house!"

She left as I was trying to squash her against the jamb with the door.

Then I was alone, deflated. I didn't feel like sending anything.

I pretended to enjoy the isolation, acting delicately towards myself, as I imagined Emily Dickinson would've done. I made tea. I took a sip. I sat the tiny, fragile cup gently on the porcelain saucer.

I felt like throwing up. I remembered that I hated tea. Why in hell was I drinking it? I guess it just seemed like the kind of thing a tender, isolated soul like myself would do.

I traipsed around the apartment, as if I knew how to do it. I picked things up — anything — the paper, a book, my penis — and gently replaced them. It was no use, I just couldn't stand it.

I decided to go to the pool, lie in the sun. I took a book in case I felt any better.

When I got to the pool, I looked around for a

lounge chair. I found one beside a sunbathing beauty of a woman who was lying on her stomach with the back of the suit undone. It was mid-morning, and the sun was still halfway up the eastern sky.

I noticed, though, that everyone was facing west, away from the sun. Most were lying on their backs.

I let this go for a while, but then it started to bug me. Finally, I had to ask the girl next to me what it was all about.

"Excuse me," I said. There was no response.

"Ex-*cuse* me," I said louder.

"Are you talking to me?" she asked with an air of disbelief.

"Yes. I am. Excuse me, but can you tell me why everyone is facing *away* from the sun?"

"Well, of course. They're tanning the backs of their toes ... And the angle is better when the sun's behind them," she continued, sensing my incomprehension.

"Oh."

It was a simple matter of fact. I guess my wife was right. I didn't have a handle on what was going on out here.

Within a few minutes, a group of people with a big radio entered the pool area. They set up right behind me. Two young women and three young guys. The women were good-looking, with fashionable hair and chic bathing suits. Their features were demure, and they held themselves with an air of class. Their manner of speaking was even more stunning.

"No fucking shit! He did *that*?"

"Yeah, he can be so nice sometimes. But then other times he's such a fucking slime."

The guys were very macho and had sandpaper voices, with what sounded like mayonnaise, which treated words like pieces of food to be savored, coating the throats for lubrication. Exactly like the kind I had to deal with in business everyday. They would be strained in suits and ties, as if their necks were about to explode and rip their shirt collars to shreds. It was odd hearing words, especially polysyllabic ones, proceed from their mouths, as if by their very natures they actually detested language and might suddenly reject it like a bad organ transplant.

Of the dozens or so people around the pool, only these five talked. On and on. And loud.

"You got anything to drink?"

"I need a drink."

"You eat anything."

"A bagel."

"Bagel's good after a long night of drinking."

"I could drink right now."

"You do anything so far?"

"Yep. I been studying. Real hard too."

They discussed studying. "You ever have to borrow a piece of paper to take notes on?" one of the guys asked.

"Yeah! Yeah!" they all agreed enthusiastically.

"I'm glad I got this Dead tape."

"Yeah."

"It's phenomenal."

"Yeah."

I picked up my book. I laid it back down again. No relief. I looked around the pool area. Very nice legs all over. I particularly noticed the frontal intersection of the upper legs at the hips.

"You ever write rough drafts?" one of the girls asked one of the guys.

"Yeah. Sometimes ten or fifteen. That's why Molly gets mad at me. And I keep editing and re-editing her stuff over and over. But she don't like it."

"That's probably why you're above her," one of the girls said.

"Don't say that to her … I check for the grammar one time. Then the syntax. But you have to read it more than once. The first time you're just reading for content."

40

I noticed that my heart was fibrillating. Don't tell me these people are *writers*? It was truly an alarming thought.

"I usually write like I talk, with parenthetical phrases," the critic went on.

I couldn't take it. I turned around to get a look at them again. The two guys were both husky, like their voices. The women were beautiful and delicate as before.

"Hey!" I heard the critic yell. He was projecting his voice further than before.

"Hey!" he threw his voice again. I tried not to move. I didn't want to show him any sign of recognition.

"Hey!" he shouted again.

"That's a Bukowski book. You're reading a Bukowski book. I *love* Bukowski, he's one of my favorites."

'Bukowski Bukowski Bukowski,' he went on.

Now I was sure of it. He was yelling at me. I didn't move a hair.

"No I really, really relate to this guy," he continued, though in a lower voice, as if he'd been talking to the girls in the first place.

"He's really one of my big influences." He went on, off, on, off, on. My hearing was shorting out. The thought of killing myself made instant entrance into my mind, along with a few possible methods of doing so. Misery loves company, but ecstasy and despair have one thing in common; they want to be left alone. The best way to find out whether or not something is really worth having is to see whether those who have it want to proselytize it or not. If they do, it's probably no good. Misery loves company.

An age-old question came to mind. In the presence of pain, stay or go? I decided to sit through it. The critic changed subjects.

"What are you getting mad for?" he asked one of the girls. "You think getting mad will help you learn it?"

No, but it will help you quit something you can't

41

do, I thought.

The Grateful Dead music droned on and on. It reminded me of Middle Eastern music: sounded like the moans of a bull having his balls twisted for hours on end.

They decided to take a swim. I took this opportunity to take a look at their papers. From where I was sitting, I could make out some university emblem. I went back and picked up a stack. I started paging through it. This was evidently the critic's finest work. Collected poems, photocopied. The first one was entitled, "To My Friend."

The friend was lying in the hospital, with tubes sticking in him. He was apparently unconscious. Sweat dripped onto the paper. Blood and guts smeared with feeling. The macho man with sensitivity routine, as found in any cop show on television. There were tubes down the nose and throat. A few good lines. Which made it hard to swallow.

The next poem was "To My Mother." I skipped it. There was a poem to his father, his girl friend, his dog, the family mixing bowl — "The Cupola Bowl," it was titled. Just about everyone and everything was represented. A real decent guy, who didn't wander far from home. I dropped the poems. They scattered on the lounge chair, which made me feel sorry for the fellow. After all, whether or not he had invented it, he had a heart.

I went back to my chair to get my things, and leave. I put on my shoes, rolled my dirty socks in the towel. I put my sunglasses on. Walked.

A few yards away, I realized I'd forgotten the Bukowski. I considered going back for it.

"Nah," I thought.

# The Moon Setting In The Dawn Of The 21st Century

Here's a guy who went to philosophy, since there was absolutely no poetry whatsoever left in his life. A perfect vacuum; well, not perfect: the suburbs, a career, with all their banal concerns. He didn't know this was the cause for his conversion. Meanwhile, as his wife would say, I don't know what these guys did for the world, this Blake and these others, I don't deny it, whatever it possibly was; that's great they left some mark or something, or changed peoples' thinking, however few, but I don't want to be *married* to someone like that, or someone who *thinks* they're like that.

It, poetry, might only be in poverty. But poverty in this country is living atop a Sheetz. Maybe some other place, some other time. That's like the same curative mentality anyway. Like exercise will do it. Fiber is what you need. No cholesterol. Oat flakes. Money. Poverty. As if in the total realm of fear, some prevention, something, some diet will save you.

Meanwhile, the demons are light-years ahead dreaming up advanced tortures and pains just for you.

But our hero, our poet-hero, is out howling at the moon. But the moon walked away — back to some primal time when she was appreciated. When the moon was real. The moon doesn't matter anymore; it doesn't mean anything, because, hell, I don't know why — the power is gone from being ignored, I guess.

But our guy (Jerry, we'll call him) keeps his wife awake at night nonetheless. With his goddamn poetry. Doesn't stop *him* that the moon, even the *moon*, gave up. This asshole's gonna keep it going — sure! Flake! Already, the workers are teaming up; at 6 a.m., most of them either have, or are currently, brushing their teeth. Jerry's hungover. From poem shock.

Get going, Jerry! Get on with it. Instead ... there! His dried-up imagination lies in stacks of paper work on his desk, at work. The salesman! The word molester! He's a professional word-knifer. He's like the walking commercial; makes your eyes water, for what? For a fucking computer chip! You're all teary eyed about *that* ... Jesus Christ! We're making communication for the 21st century ... shit like that. Well, what do you want the guy to do, eat rehydrated soup like all the other suckers? He's not gonna give in to their notion. No. He'll be disguised with a lot of gadgets.

Aside from that, he conjures a lot of philosophy. No, not just opinions like other stupid big mouths; he goes into the *books* of philosophy. The real heavies at that. Need I name them? No. Because he wouldn't breath a word himself.

But Jerry is aware of the vast chasm between poetry and philosophy. He knows, as one nut-cake who had the time and notion to think about it, Karl Shapiro, said, philosophy is the abstraction of experience, poetry, the materialization. What kind of guy are you, Jerry? Where are you coming from? His wife could not care much less about such distinctions. If they folded and kamikaze'd into mutual self-destruction, she wouldn't sleep any worse. The whole goddamn thing was selfish, she said, and if Jerry never wrote another goddamn word, all right, good! If he one day *did* become immortalized, his would make an interesting biography.

He could hear her, imagined her voice in his head: What the hell are you worried about the *moon* for? God I live with a complete nut case! Who in the hell sits awake worrying about the f---king moon? (She had class; she never deleted the "ING" sound.) This is what he heard, as she lay, still sleeping.

It *was* frightening, even to Jerry himself. Here he was, the provider for four, sitting up, completely lurid. It was okay for other Geralds, like Hopkins, who was a real nut; lived alone, a priest or something. He could sit or stand around getting "shook like foil" from suns and moons, or whatever he wanted. But Jerry was busy. He had a lot to do.

Not the least of which was to take a shower, and get his shirt pressed, and get to work. He could leave poetry to his son, who was better at it anyway.

"Look, Daddy," he said pointing to the sky nights before; "the whole future moves. The future is MOVING! The future's in the sky!" That's exactly what he said. Jerry's son. The kid was right, wasn't he? The future, the whole thing, like a block, keeps shifting ahead. When you think you have it nailed, the frame changes. And the moon moves too. It's gone. Obsolete.

And there's nothing all the poets in the world, with all their little magazines, can do about it.

# The D.

I picked up a piece of darkness. One night when I went out walking. I looked between two tall buildings. This sliver of darkness jumped out. I wrestled with it. No use. I was overcome. It was attached. So I came down with this darkness, which formed a second eye-lid over my third eye. Know what I mean? You know the third eye, the one your mind sees with?

Naturally I started thinking there was something wrong with me. You weren't supposed to be aware of it. The third eye. It was supposed to be clear. But now that I had this reptilian-like filmy growth tissue over it, things changed. There was more shade now. Now the human habitat looked insufficient. And grimy. And robbed of something. I guess it's how the zoo must appear to the captive animal. Fake. I strained to see things as before. No avail.

I was staying in a hotel in downtown Boston at the time. The best hotel in town, in my opinion. The Westin, Copley Square. An elaborate creation of marble brass and arrogance. Now it seemed like Las Vegas. A great big hoax phoenix. Deprived as the world actually is, I wanted only shacks. I went to bed. It was 7:00 at night.

I woke up at three in the morning. I had been dreaming of my mother. We were having a conversation in the twilight. She sat across from me in a trailer beside a construction site. The moon sat in the window. The one beside her head. She poured me a cup of black coffee. I drank it gratefully while we talked silently. And the volume rose. I got up and took a shower.

I ordered a pot of coffee from room service. An East Indian answered. It was four in the morning. A perfect strangeness. I thought he asked me how my mother was. I'm sure he hadn't. How many cups? he asked me. I knew I had to see her. She was trying to tell me something.

At least until the sun came up, and everything cleared up to nothing.

I grabbed an early flight to Orlando. I had some business there anyhow. I could make it up if I had to. There was rarely any physical means unavailable, really. I spent the day in Orlando. I went to Disney World. It was fun in Disney World by myself, though not the usual fun. Then I picked up a rental car and drove northeast to my mother's. I had to ask her something. It was about the darkness.

I showed up. She was frightened to see me. Jesus why was I there? Oh My God What Brought You Here? It was as if I'd slipped a gear in Actual Time on my Timex Skialthom watch, which is good down to one hundred and forty leagues under the sea. Not to mention Sea Level. She was as white as a ghost. Or was I seeing things? She looked to have absolutely no blood circulation in her face What So Ever. I thought for a minute she was dead and I was alive in Death or was I dead in Life and she was alive in Death. Oh well. Every second barely jerked along. On my second hand, it must've been sticking. That's the way it was with my mother.

That's the way it was with my mother.

It took me thirteen hours to get to the point. I never got there. The darkness, the D. as I came to refer to it, didn't have a point. But I beat around the bush, all around it. I tried to describe it to her. She was not surprised in the least, when we finally got to it. It was to her as though we'd really gotten nowhere. It was all the same. It was twilight. We were sitting in the trailer, in the trailer park. The sun was coming a crack up in the window. Beside her. It wasn't unusual to her to be talking like this in the twilight. She could go to sleep in the middle of a circus too. Nor was the D.

It was my inheritance, she said. The D. My inheritance. It's inherited, she said. She talked about it right in front of it, as if it weren't even there.

47

And also, as if it weren't strange. Could we be talking about the same thing? The D., this nebulous cloudy thing, inherited? Uncle George had it too? Are you sure? Oh yes, Andrew, Uncle George, and your Aunt Margaret, your grandfather, my father, even your father, they all had it.

Why? Why wasn't I told about this before? I asked her. Why not? she said. Why should you be spared? You think you're better than life? Where do you come off, really, Andrew? she said.

But somehow my mother, she was always in the conclusion, and me, I was always in the orifice. Nothing was stranger to me than that, but to her, nothing more perfectly natural. When my head came out on the carpet, in the trailer, in the trailer park. To her, it was no surprise. But when I arrived years later at the door of the trailer, she had a mild heart attack. But hours later, when my head came out, D. and all, no surprise at all.

She poured me another cup of coffee. My nerves were having an erection. My mother wasn't alarmed. She'd seen it before. I think I've seen it before, she said. I've seen it before, she said. Things weren't getting any better. To her, it was all the same. I wondered if she wondered if I wondered whether I might punch out that glass beside her head and cut my throat across the trailer? I told her that. She hadn't wondered. But she wasn't surprised either.

But it was Faith. That's what got her through, she said. Through what, I said, why did we have to get *through* something? What was the It we had to get through? It was natural to her. Faith. Why? Because the D. was natural too. I Turn It Over, she said. I Turn It Over, she said. I Turn It Over. And over and over and over. That's the way she cooked eggs too. Scrambled. NO WONDER I WAS NUTS, I thought. I turn it over to God, she said. Because I can't handle it. I let Him handle it, she said, I can't handle it myself.

48

Well, that's what keeps me from cutting my throat, honestly, Andrew. Otherwise, you're right, I may as well slice my neck right now.

But that's not what I said, I said. I didn't say that, I said. I didn't say that. I didn't say Otherwise You Should Cut Your Throat.

I didn't say it. Really I didn't. I didn't say she should do it. Or I should do it. I just thought she should be surprised. I thought she should know.

# The Monk

Lying on the couch, he looks out the sliding glass door through the vertical blinds, at the gnarled wet trees; he listens to the plops of rain on the porch, wanting nothing more, but he turns his head to look behind, where through the small window he sees the wall of the building which adjoins his at a right angle. The red brick institutional walls, the long series of parallel windows with tinged yellowed blinds, and the somber, and staid and blackened windowsills — he gets up and goes into the kitchen. He pauses in front of the refrigerator. Between himself and the refrigerator he sees a stream of radio waves, FM modality. He tunes in: metronomic thumping, definitely designed to drive him mad and into a rage. He switches out. This time by contemplating what sits behind the metal door of the refrigerator. A long, deserted beach, strewn with petrified wood, replete with an undercurrent of symphonic thrashing of waves. On a rock, just seconds ago two hundred yards away, now right in front of him, a chilly glass with beads of condensation. A split lime-wedge on the lip of the glass, with a thin straw. He draws the gin and tonic through the straw, and walks back to the couch. He stares out at the trees, barely noticing the noise in the kitchen — of paper bags crinkling, and plastic and glass bottles being shuttled. But he is no less soothed by them. It's the calm that comes when final solutions are reached. Such is the feeling derived by a mendicant. The provisions are prepared.

Now he is confronted with a street and subsumed in a peculiar set of circumstances, which, set against the backdrop of the trees, and the rain falling on the wooden porch, and the silent character of the side of the building, which he now turns his head around to look at again, thrusts him into the burden of resolving an incongruity. The action in which he is forced to become involved is absurdist by way of the trees: blatant characters who purport to threaten him in some way, though it is probably in the abstract. Now he sees it; it has to do with some terror they will impose. And what they threaten him with is personal extinction in so much as he will not stand up to the mental torture. But he must go with them. Otherwise something will have been left undone. And this is the problem. But it's over before they go in. It ends on the steps outside, the narrow and sloping and worn-down steps that lead up to the door from the sidewalk into the (?). But it was certainly daytime because the clouds lining the sky were blue and molten gray; the effect was that of an eclipse. But somehow they managed to affect the torture without entering the building.

And he hasn't at all noticed until now the two friars standing over him at the end of the couch, who appear to be patiently waiting for a response to some question. What was the question? But their kind faces have remnants of the menacing nightclub goers on them. Do you want a drink? They are asking him. They are perfectly happy to bring it to him. He sees the evil has gotten into them too. Their complexions have a green tone where the snake shows through the translucent flesh. He nods in acceptance of the drink, doing so as the prevention of the other alternative, which must be death. His drink is replenished, and he is completely unaware of the hand or the body behind the hand that delivers it, only the trees and their ultraviolet halos glazed over them like purple wigs, which are trimmed from time to time by an almost imperceptibly mild wind, which frays particles away like cloth threads. And he hears a conversation going on. The speech is so chopped that phrases and words even are broken and exchanged between two parties, who cannot get enough and become increasingly frenzied and thereby shred language further and further into pieces. The two characters are desperate and wear old bits of woolen clothing in shades of gray, which they seem to want to exchange continuously in a rapid fervor, along with words. Or are they exchanging pills from their brown pill bottles?

The monks resume the singing, a long moaning which stretches out into infinity. He sees the sound waves trail off around the bell tower … a huge engulfing fear of the endless agony that the singing portrays. The monks, he knows, are only monks in posturing. The charade is kept up. It is partly connected to the nightclub goers. The Gregorian chants reverberate around the monastery. And the hushed talking, which he hears coming from rooms in the complex, in the nightclub on the other side of the walls.

And these pictures of the nightclub seep into his dreaming, as he currently falls asleep on the couch. The gin-and-tonic glass falls out of his hand and shatters on the grimy dance floor. The club is run-down, yet its frequency is high pitched nonetheless. The regulars display an uncanny pride, and though the place is probably abandoned, six or seven men turn on him in the bar as his glass shatters. They each wear mustaches, cowboy hats, denim jeans, and boots. The filth around them seems to be a source of hostility toward this stranger, whom they imagine to be indignant over it. But now he realizes that only one of the six (or seven) men is actually confronting him. The others had only turned at the crashing sound of glass, and have turned away and back into their silent conversations, indifferent. This is the wrong crowd for the nightclub, he remembers, and he quickly begins to erase them. But as usual, he has a bit of trouble changing the situation, and the one cowboy gets closer.

He is temporarily unable to determine the difference between the cowboy and the monk, who cleans up the glass beside the couch. The monks keep a secret. That is why they don't talk. Some of them are inveterate

Nazis, expert in silent torture. They keep secret dogs under the chapel of the monastery, which of course accounts for all the extra cooking. They've taken over the Garden of Eden due largely to the fact that they have a certain edge when it comes to spiritual matters. But whether they keep the secret of evil, or of good, it's evil that they keep it hidden. That's the reason for the dogs, in case anyone, like the FBI for instance, should try to uncover it. Of course, they could find it, but when they did, they'd destroy it before knowing what it was, because they're vulgar compared to the monks.

And that is why the monks keep him hidden here. The drinks are meant to keep the transmissions to a minimum. They know that, from the consultant. The consultant of course is consigned to them by the government, and a few government officials, who are involved in graft, have made a special agreement, clandestine and illegal, with the monastery, and it is this deal that has him here. What the government and the monastery are unaware of is something that he cannot even think of; in fact, already a danger is presented. Thinking of it, even acknowledging that there is an "it," will virtually originate a transmission. And he has asked me that this not be dwelt upon for a second longer.

But he has determined that another reason for the silence, and perhaps the primary one, has to do with the radio reception. But again, the purpose of the radio signals is a sort of advanced torture, a kind of a torture, which, because of its incredible subtlety, would not be a torture at all, except to a very distinct kind of person. And this general imperceptibility only adds to the peculiarity of it, and makes it torture.

Now another drink is brought in, containing what it has in it is hard to tell, as the taste is a blanched pale shade of … (medicine?) He is in the dark corridor, which leads somewhere, but he doesn't remember: he turns the corner, and to another corridor, and so on. The halls are of marble floors, and drab pale painted walls, some yellow, some green. Although the general rule is silence, he hears faint echoes of voices. Through infrequent windows, he sees the small gardens, which are enclosed by the outside walls of the angled corridors, and are open to the sky, motionless. Small rose bushes, violets, hyacinths, irises, and Black-eyed Susans form the centerpieces surrounded by the trapezoidal patches of grass, which are bordered by concrete benches. These are the enclosed, captured remnants of the Garden of Eden, which the monks guard fastidiously and with extreme covetousness, thumbing the wood studded nooses and murmuring curses at the nightclub goers.

Whom, they are convinced, he brought in. Which accounts for the drinks. Or, what else could account for them? He has a hunch that the monks and the nightclub goers are actually the same people, who merely alternate costumes. And this would mean that the whole thing is really a plot, which he is meant to witness for some reason. Although it is intended, perhaps, that he think just this. Are they trying to convince him that he committed some evil act that they are actually responsible for? That would explain the intermittent presence of the consultant, to whom he is to confess, who would then take him to the F.B.I., permitting the consultant to release the monks, who could then resume their roles as the nightclub goers.

Although another possibility occurs to him as well. And this has something to do with his ability to advance their knowledge regarding spiritual matters, although dousing him with drinks would seem to preclude this. The intermediary role of the consultant would be lost as well.

But why is the ladder still standing up outside? There's a ladder, stemming from the ground to the second floor balcony of his apartment. Naturally, he's not going to go down it. The whole world would collapse if he did. He expects someone to come up the ladder, burst through the sliding glass door, and fire shots at him.

He is so afraid that he is actually like a skinned animal turned inside out. Yet he knows that he is only a victim of these threats because he is transmitting the fear to the killers. They receive the signals, much like a smell that doesn't travel to the senses but suddenly arrives in the mind — and his entire mind is no more than a transmitter, which means that his being is just a transformer. His body is the physical transistor, and his mind is the invisible waves (except to him) that the body creates. Whereas, the monks have other purposes. They emit something of a slower, larger wave, which grants them the feeling of time, and events going on in time. While he is pitched higher, extremely high, such that all events are simultaneous, and do not require any physical existence. But the monks require even further proof of things, beyond their physical existence. That's why they repeat things over and over, like the singing, as if singing once were not enough. Once something is there, it is there. But apparently they do not know this yet. They are committing static to the atmosphere, which is only serving to clutter the perceptual field. Of course this may very well be their intention. And likewise they are drawing his attention to the utter emptiness; by filling space with the same vibrations continuously, the blankness of the subtext is thereby highlighted, much as a Zen character diminishes the depth of field of the background, leaving a horizontal plane, which means he is trapped. "Trappist." He knows that much, that he is flat. That the scene is frozen without area beyond a single dimension.

## The Storm

I looked over. His head hanging. The pistol in his hand, still pointed at his stomach. I kept driving. I didn't want to stop right away. Figured it would wake him. His head jerked up and his eyes rolled around under the lids. "Shit," I thought, "he's coming to."

His chubby little vanilla, three-year-old-boy hands looked cute holding the toy gun.

"Christ, how could I ever yell at this kid?" I thought.

But I was depressed. Not about the kid, although he made me feel guilty about it. Not more than three minutes after we were in the car, he'd gone out, as if the huge spiraling funnel of my emotions had drawn the spirit right out of him. That's one thing about children. They give you their soul without a second thought.

A spring storm was brewing. Treetops swayed in the wind. The song playing on the tape deck was about a storm. I drove.

I kept driving.

I'd barely noticed that I'd gotten onto an unfamiliar road. I paid no attention at all, moving along without thinking. Everything was just a quiet darkening, a few people standing on the sides of the road, stuck in time.

After a while we were outside the suburb, in the country, under a tunnel of over-hanging trees. The car wound around the curves, as if by itself.

The rain started. Slow at first, but then, crash, the whole place was flooded. Surges of water banged down on the car. I looked over. He was still asleep. The storm didn't matter to him — he still had his gun. The water rushed nearly a foot high on the road, as the car forged through against the current.

The headlights, cast into the spray of water and mist, projected a luminescent ghost in front of the car, and the steam built up on the windshield faster than my hand and the defroster could clear.

He was still out, not even a word of sleep-talk.

I turned back to the windshield. Wiping, wiping. My arm going frantically on the glass. I zipped the window down. A wave slapped against the side of my head. I zipped it back up.

I heard his tiny, high-pitched voice, soft and faint, as if made of a vibration of a soft, white water.

"Daddy? Are we in a car-wash?"

"Huh?" I said, making sure the voice wasn't in my head before answering.

"Daddy, are we driving in your dream?"

I pulled the car into a gully on the side of the road. We sat and waited out the dream.

Then I turned the car around, and retraced the tracks. The molten clouds were breaking up, moving in a fast-forward movie. My son and I sat with our heads still and erect, as if they'd just poked through the clouds. Everything was clear.

We didn't talk; I looked over at him, his reverent silence. It was too early to make judgments about anything. I couldn't remember what exactly had been bothering me.

I decided this would be my religion, tracing his silence, straight to the heart.

# About the Author

Michael Rectenwald, Ph.D. has taught writing and cultural history at New York University since 2008. He received a B.A. in English from the University of Pittsburgh, an M.A. from Case Western Reserve University, and a Ph.D. in Literary and Cultural Studies from Carnegie Mellon University. At age twenty, Michael was an apprentice poet to Allen Ginsberg at the Jack Kerouac School of Disembodied Poetics, at Naropa Institute in Boulder, Colorado.

In addition to publishing numerous essays in his field of cultural studies and the history of science, he writes occasional poetry, fiction, screenplays, and political commentary. In 1991, he published the *Eros of the Baby Boom Eras* (poetry). His website is at www.michaelrectenwald.com. His political commentary can be found at www.legitgov.org.